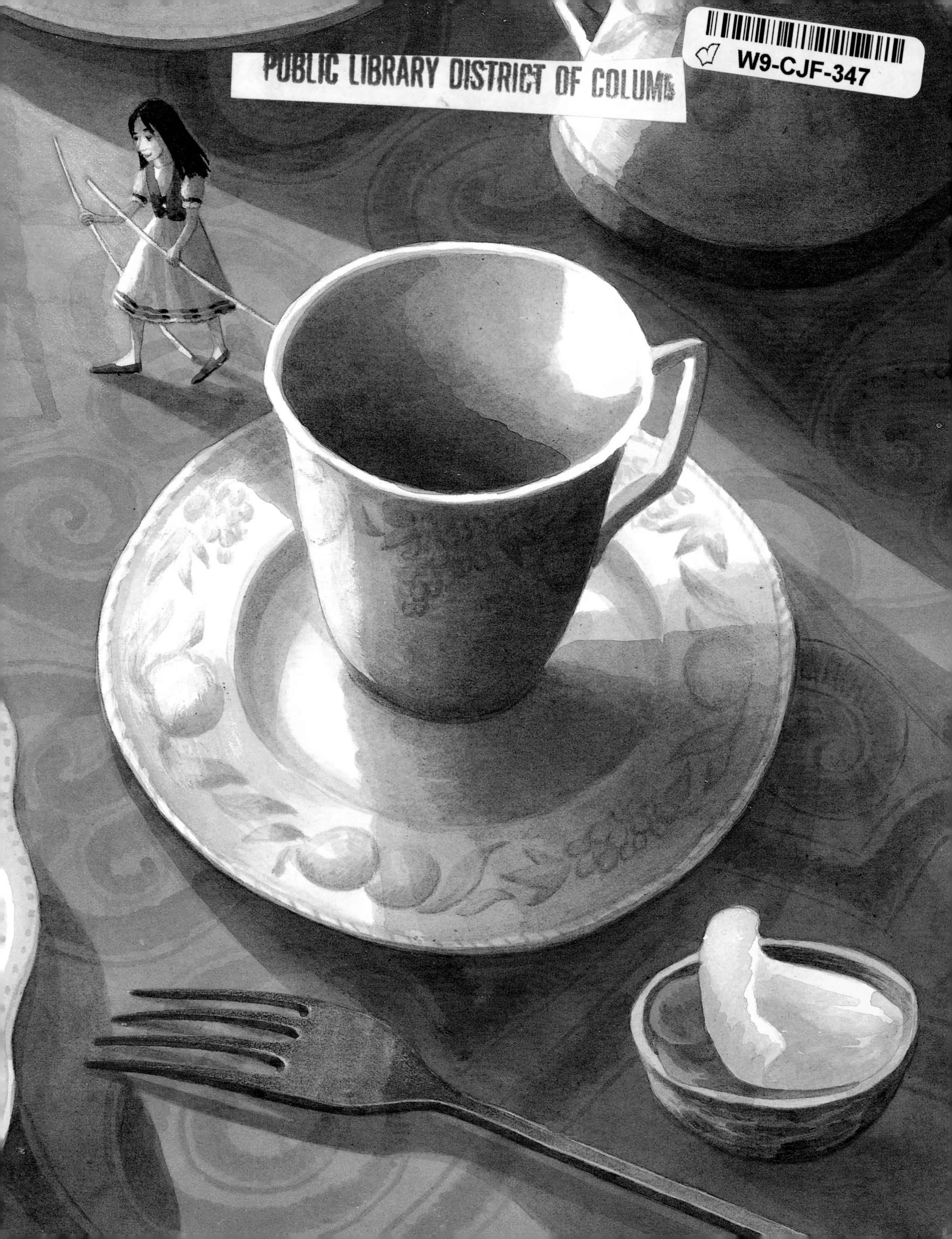

**MARGARET K. McELDERRY BOOKS**
25 YEARS • 1972–1997

Margaret K. McElderry Books
An imprint of
Simon & Schuster Children's Publishing Division
1230 Avenue of the Americas
New York, New York 10020

First United States edition 1997

Text copyright © 1996 by Jane Falloon
Illustrations copyright © 1996 by Emma Chichester Clark
First published in Great Britain in 1996 by
Pavilion Books Limited, London

Designed by Elizabeth McTernan
The text of this book is set in Sabon.

Printed in Hong Kong

2 4 6 8 10 9 7 5 3 1

Library of Congress Cataloging-in-Publication Data

Falloon, Jane.
Thumbelina / retold by Jane Falloon; illustrated by Emma
Chichester Clark.—1st U.S. ed.
p. cm.
Summary: After being kidnapped by a toad, a beautiful girl
no bigger than a thumb has a series of dreadful experiences
and makes many animal friends before meeting a fairy
prince just her size.
[1. Fairy tales.] I. Chichester Clark, Emma, ill. II.
Andersen, H. C. (Hans Christian), 1805-1875.
Tommelise. III. Title.
PZ8.F189Th  1997
[Fic]—dc20
96 - 1422 CIP AC
ISBN 0-689-81181-0

# THUMBELINA

*Retold by Jane Falloon*
*Illustrated by Emma Chichester Clark*

Margaret K. McElderry Books

Quite a long time ago, there lived a young farmer's wife.
She desperately wanted a child of her very own, but she
didn't know where she could find one. She decided to visit
a wise woman who lived nearby to ask her advice.

"Could you please tell me," she said to the old woman,
"where I can find a child of my very own?"

"Well," said the wise woman, "you've come to the right
place. I have a grain of corn here—it's magic. Take it
home, plant it in a flowerpot, and see what happens."

"Oh, thank you," cried the farmer's wife, and she gave the old woman a silver penny. She raced home and planted the grain of corn in a flowerpot, and no sooner had she done so than the seed started to grow. It grew amazingly fast, and in a few minutes a flower bud appeared at the top of the stem. It looked something like a closed-up tulip.

"How pretty it is!" exclaimed the farmer's wife, and in her excitement she bent over and kissed its red and yellow petals. Just as she did so, there was a popping sound and the tulip opened. There, sitting in the middle of it, was a tiny girl. She was very, very pretty, and exactly the same size as your thumb—and as the farmer's wife's thumb too. So she decided to call her Thumbelina.

She gave Thumbelina half a walnut shell, beautifully polished, to sleep in. The mattress was made of violet petals, and the sheets were rose petals. Thumbelina slept in this cradle at night, but in the daytime the farmer's wife let her play on the kitchen table. She made a pool for her out of a plate, with flowers floating around the edge.

Thumbelina sailed on the pool in a tulip petal. She had two oars made of white horsehairs, and as she rowed around she sang to herself in a sweet, tiny voice.

Just the girl for my son!

One night, when she was asleep in her walnut-shell cradle, a huge, ugly toad jumped into the house through a broken windowpane. She hopped up onto the table where Thumbelina lay asleep and goggled down at her.

"Just the girl for my son," she croaked to herself, and without more ado she grabbed the walnut shell with Thumbelina inside and hopped off with it through the window.

At the bottom of the garden was the toad's home, on the muddy edge of a great river. The toad's son looked just like his mother; warty and wrinkled and dreadfully unattractive. All he could do when he saw Thumbelina was croak idiotically.

"Don't make so much noise, or you'll wake her up!" hissed his mother. "She could easily run away; she's as light as thistledown. Let's anchor her out in the middle of the stream on a water-lily leaf. She won't be able to escape from there—and meanwhile, we can get her room ready for when she marries you."

The old toad chose a big water-lily leaf, far out in the middle of the water, and swam out with the walnut shell, with Thumbelina still sleeping inside.

Early the next morning the tiny girl woke up and looked with horror at the water all around her. She cried most despairingly at her piteous plight. How was she to escape?

Meanwhile, the old toad was trying to make her muddy home pretty for the little girl who was to be her son's bride. She decorated it with reeds and the petals of yellow water lilies; then she called her son and they swam out together to Thumbelina on her leaf. They meant to take away her walnut shell for her new room. The old toad made a sort of curtsy to her in the water, and then introduced her son.

"This is my handsome boy, who is to be your bridegroom—and we have made a wonderful home for you down in the mud," she rasped.

The bridegroom-to-be could only utter a ridiculous croak.

The mother and son seized her little bed and swam off with it, leaving poor Thumbelina in tears on the leaf. She hated the thought of living with the old toad in the mud and marrying her dreadful son. Luckily, some little fishes swimming nearby had overheard what the toad had said.

They poked their heads out of the water to have a look at Thumbelina. Of course, they thought her wonderfully pretty and charming, and they were shocked to think of her having to marry the toad. They realized they had to help her somehow. If they could gnaw through the stem of the leaf she was standing on, it would float away down the river and carry her to safety. And that is just what happened.

Thumbelina sailed downstream on her leaf; past towns and villages, on and on, out of that country and into another one, far away. The birds perching in the nearby trees watched her go by and twittered to each other with delight at her prettiness. Quite soon she was joined by a white butterfly. It fluttered around her as she floated along and then settled on her leaf. She felt almost happy. She had escaped from the toads, the sun was shining, and she had a companion to share her journey. Thumbelina decided to tie the butterfly to the leaf with her ribbon; now they went much faster. She loved standing up on the leaf as it cut swiftly through the water like a skiff.

Near the forest was a cornfield, but there was no corn to be found, just sharp stubble sticking up from the frozen ground. Thumbelina was walking, dazed and shivering, through these spiky stems, which looked as big as tree trunks to her, when she saw a little doorway in the ground. It was the home of a field mouse. Pitifully cold and hungry, she knocked timidly.

"Could you possibly spare me a grain or two of corn? I haven't eaten anything for two days," she faltered.

The field mouse, luckily, was kind and good. "You poor little thing," she said. "You must come in at once and have something to eat."

She had a warm, comfortable house: a whole room full of corn and a lovely kitchen and larder.

"If you will do my housework for me, and amuse me by telling me stories, you may stay here for the winter," she said. So Thumbelina thankfully settled in with her.

you poor little thing!

Mrs. Fieldmouse told Thumbelina about her friend, the mole. "He'll be coming to see us very soon; he comes most days. He's very rich, and he's always dressed most becomingly in black velvet. You should have him for your husband. He will love listening to your stories because, poor thing, he's blind."

Thumbelina didn't think she wanted to marry a mole. Even though his house stretched on and on under the ground and he was rich and clever, she hated the thought of living in the dark with no flowers or sunshine.

When he came visiting, she obediently sang songs to him, and the mole promptly fell in love with her because of her beautiful voice.

He invited her and Mrs. Fieldmouse to visit him by way of a special passage he had dug from his house to hers, and told them not to be upset when they passed the dead bird. It had already been buried there when he made the passage.

The mole lit the way for them through the long tunnel with a piece of glowing charcoal. When they came to the bird, he reached up and made a hole in the roof with his long nose to let in some light.

The bird was a swallow. Thumbelina looked at his beautiful dark shining head, his red throat and dark blue wings. When she saw him looking so huddled and cold, she felt terribly sad. She loved birds, remembering how they had sung to her as she drifted down the river. But the

field mouse and the mole were quite heartless about him.

"Thank goodness my children won't be birds," said the mole. "All they can do is sing, and they're bound to starve to death in winter."

"Quite right," said Mrs. Fieldmouse. "What good does singing do them? It doesn't get them anything to eat."

Thumbelina said nothing, but when they weren't looking she knelt down and kissed the swallow's closed eyes. *Maybe he's the one I heard singing so sweetly last summer,* she thought. *He made me so happy then with his song.*

The mole closed up the hole he had made in the roof and took them back to their home.

That night Thumbelina could not sleep. She got up quietly and went and found some soft wool and some hay and wove a warm blanket. Then she crept back down the passage and wrapped it gently around the dead bird.

"Good-bye, lovely swallow," she whispered. "Thank you for your beautiful singing." Then she sadly leaned her cheek against the bird's soft breast. As she did so, what did she hear?

A very soft beating sound. It was the bird's heart. He was not dead, but sleeping—hibernating, as some creatures do in winter. The warmth had revived him. For a minute Thumbelina was terrified, because the swallow was so much bigger than she was, but very bravely she managed to wrap him up more warmly.

The next night she went back to see how he was. The swallow was able to open his eyes but was still very weak. When he saw Thumbelina standing there, lit by her piece of glowing charcoal, he spoke to her.

"Thank you, my dear child," he said. "You have warmed me up wonderfully well. Soon I'll be able to fly again."

"But not yet!" Thumbelina said anxiously. "It's much too cold outside. You must stay in here where it's warm, and I'll look after you."

She brought him water to drink, and he explained to her how he had been left behind when his companions flew south. He had hurt one of his wings and couldn't keep up with them. He had fallen to the ground and remembered nothing more after that.

All through the winter Thumbelina secretly cared for the swallow. She didn't tell the others because she knew they didn't like him. But when spring came, and the sun's warmth could be felt even underground, Thumbelina had to open the hole in the roof to let him fly away.

"Why not come with me?" he asked her. "You could sit on my back and fly far away with me."

Thumbelina longed to say yes, but knew that the field mouse would be very upset if she left. Watching the swallow fly away, her eyes filled with tears.

"Good-bye, good-bye, you good, kind child," whistled the swallow as he flew up into the sunshine and away, away, high over the forest trees.

So Thumbelina was left behind in the darkness. To make matters worse, the mole was determined to marry her and the field mouse thought it an excellent plan as well. She insisted on preparing for the wedding, so they settled down to make all the things Thumbelina would need as a bride. Four spiders came in, and all through the summer they spun and wove and sewed for Thumbelina's trousseau. The dreary old mole came to visit every night and kept talking about the wedding. But whenever she had a chance, Thumbelina would go and peep through the great stalks of corn above the field mouse's nest. She would gaze up at the blue sky and the light, and long to see her friend the swallow again.

Nonsense! How dare you!

Eventually autumn arrived, and everything was ready for the wedding.

"Only four weeks to go!" chortled Mrs. Fieldmouse.

"But I don't want to marry him!" lamented Thumbelina.

"Nonsense. How dare you say that! Such a handsome bridegroom in his beautiful black velvet. And so rich! Any more of this and you'll regret it, my girl." The field mouse looked really fierce for a moment.

So the wedding day drew nearer. At last the mole came to

take Thumbelina deep down into the earth, where she'd never see the light again. Before she went with him, she ran up to the cornfield for the last time and lifted her little arms high in the air.

"Good-bye, sunshine," she cried desolately. "Good-bye, good-bye."

There was a red poppy growing near her, and she flung her arms around it. "Good-bye, poppy," she said. "If you see the swallow, give him my love."

Suddenly she heard a soft whistling above her. It was the swallow. Just by chance, he was flying past. He immediately swooped down beside her.

"Oh, Swallow!" she exclaimed. "It's really you at last! But I'm in such trouble. I'm supposed to marry the mole this very day! And then I'll have to live underground for the rest of my life and never see the sun again." She couldn't help crying bitterly as she told him.

The swallow watched her gently. "Please don't cry," he said. "I'll help you. It's the season for me to fly south again, and this time I *will* take you with me. You can tie yourself onto my back, and we'll fly south together.

"We'll fly far across the mountains to a land where there are wonderful flowers and it's always warm and sunny. Let me save you, as you once saved me when I was lying frozen in the dark."

   Thumbelina gazed at him, too happy to say anything for
a minute. She knew that this time she must go with him.
Then she put her arms around his neck and murmured,
"Of course I'll go with you." Quickly she climbed up onto
his back and tied herself to his feathers with her ribbon.

Up into the air they flew together.

Away they went, over forests and lakes, seas and mountains. Eventually they came to the warm southern lands of the sun.

Thumbelina looked down, and there below her were lush vineyards and groves of orange and lemon trees. As they flew lower she could see gardens full of flowers. The scent from the flowers and sweet herbs wafted up to her. Little children were running about, chasing brightly patterned butterflies. Above her it seemed as if the sky were twice as high and six times as blue as she had ever known it.

Then, ahead, there slowly came into sight a shining white marble palace with pillars and turrets, and, beside it, a great blue lake, where the white palace's reflection danced and sparkled.

"We have reached my home," the swallow said as they drifted down to land. "You can live here too. We shall find a flower for you to live in. You'll be safe and happy here."

"How wonderful—look, I can see one now!" exclaimed Thumbelina, pointing to a tall white lily growing between some pieces of a marble column. So the swallow flew down, and she carefully climbed off his back onto one of its broad green leaves.

Then she saw him. Sitting in the middle of the flower was a tiny man looking down at her. He looked almost as if he were made of glass—delicate and transparent. He had wings like a dragonfly and a gold crown on his head. What's more, he was exactly the same size as Thumbelina. She looked around and saw that all the other flowers had tiny people in them too.

"Don't you think he's handsome?" Thumbelina murmured softly to the swallow. The King of the Flowers—for that is who he was—felt frightened for a moment when he saw the huge swallow. But then he saw Thumbelina. She was the most beautiful girl he had ever seen. So, without more ado, he took off his crown and put it on her head. And then what do you think he did? He went down on one knee, on the leaf, and asked her to marry him. Oh yes, and he asked her her name.

"Thumbelina."

"Thumbelina? It isn't a nice enough name for you. I shall give you another one. I shall call you Maya. Maya is the name of the Queen of the Flowers, and that is what you'll be if you marry me. So, will you?"

Thumbelina looked at him. Here, at last, was a husband she could really love and admire. She thought for a second about the others who had asked her: the dreadful toad and the dreary mole.

"Of course I will," she said.

At these words, all the flower people came flying toward them carrying presents for her. The best of all was a pair of dragonfly wings, just like the King's, so she could fly as well!

The swallow sang most sweetly from his nest in the palace wall above her, wishing her happiness. But his heart was sad because he loved her too, and always wanted to be with her.

And do you know how I know this? Later on, the swallow flew back to the cold northern lands and perched on my windowsill. He told me the whole long story of his beautiful little friend, my Thumbelina, and how she lived happily ever after.